the littlest SMOKE DETECTOR

By
Dave Brozman

Illustrated by: Jesus Rodriguez

AuthorHouse™
1663 Liberty Drive, Suite 200
Bloomington, IN 47403
www.authorhouse.com
Phone: 1-800-839-8640

AuthorHouse™ UK Ltd.
500 Avebury Boulevard
Central Milton Keynes, MK9 2BE
www.authorhouse.co.uk
Phone: 08001974150

First published by AuthorHouse 9/19/2006

ISBN: 1-4259-6096-0 (sc)

Printed in the United States of America
Bloomington, Indiana

This book is printed on acid-free paper.

Bloomington, IN Milton Keynes, UK

authorHOUSE®

To Deb
you inspire me

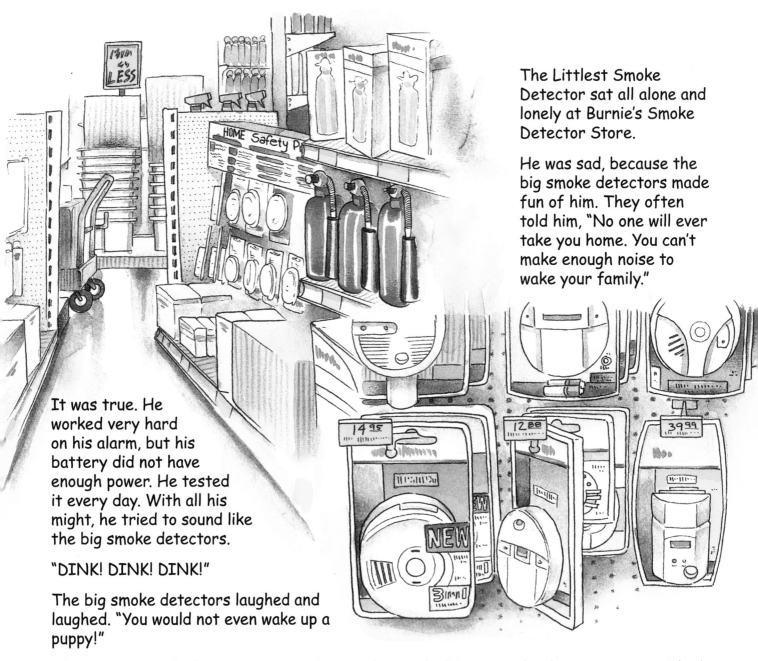

The Littlest Smoke Detector sat all alone and lonely at Burnie's Smoke Detector Store.

He was sad, because the big smoke detectors made fun of him. They often told him, "No one will ever take you home. You can't make enough noise to wake your family."

It was true. He worked very hard on his alarm, but his battery did not have enough power. He tested it every day. With all his might, he tried to sound like the big smoke detectors.

"DINK! DINK! DINK!"

The big smoke detectors laughed and laughed. "You would not even wake up a puppy!"

The Littlest Smoke Detector watched every day as the bigger smoke detectors were picked from the shelf. He knew that they would be given a new home and a very important job. Smoke detectors protect everyone from smoke and fire. This is because a smoke detector _never_ sleeps!

Then one day, when he was sure no one would ever take him home, it happened! The Martin children came into the store. Robbie and Jill were looking for a birthday present for their father. "What shall we buy?" said Robbie

"How about a fire extinguisher?" said Jill.

"We already have one in the garage and in the kitchen," said Robbie.

"I know," exclaimed Jill. "Dad was going to replace the smoke detector in the hall because it's ten years old."

"Great idea," said Robbie.

As Jill picked up the Littlest Smoke Detector, she asked, "how about this one?"

"Looks a little puny to me," said Robbie.

Jill held the Littlest Smoke Detector. "Let me push the test button. I'm sure it will be just fine."

This was the Littlest Smoke Detector's big chance. If he ever wanted to protect this family from smoke, he had to make a big noise. He gathered all the power his little battery could muster. Jill reached for the test button. This was it!

"DINK! DINK! DINK!"

The Littlest Smoke Detector was so embarrassed. He could hear all the other smoke detectors laughing.

"We should just call him Dink, because that's all the noise he will ever make," said one of the big smoke detectors.

"He not only looks puny, he even sounds puny," said Robbie.

The Littlest Smoke Detector felt so sad. All he wanted to do was crawl back on the shelf and hide behind the big smoke detectors. Suddenly, Jill said, "Well, I like him, and I think he will do a great job!"

"Okay, but dad may bring him back if he can't wake us up," said Robbie.

"Don't worry, this smoke detector will be a very important part of our family fire-escape plan," said Jill. As the Littlest Smoke Detector was being put into the shopping bag, he was sure he could hear someone say, "Good luck, little guy." The words of encouragement came from the smoke detector shelf.

The children could not wait for their father's birthday party. They had saved all the money from their allowance to buy a gift. "We even got change back," said Robbie.

"Yes, now we can put a big bow on the box. This will be the best present, ever!" said Jill.

After cake and ice cream, it was time to open presents. "Open our present first," said Jill.

Mr. Martin looked at the small box with the big bow. "Could this be a new tie?" he asked.

"It's a present the whole family can use," said Robbie. Mr. Martin carefully removed the bow and opened the box. A big smile crossed his face. "This <u>is</u> a gift the whole family can use."

After the rest of the gifts were opened, Robbie could not wait to install the new smoke detector. "Dad, can we put up our new smoke detector?"

"Okay, son, go to the garage and get the stepladder," said Mr. Martin. With a screwdriver in hand, Mr. Martin took the old smoke detector off the ceiling. "Do you think this is a good place for the smoke detector?" asked Mr. Martin.

"Sure," said Jill, "it's high on the ceiling. Smoke always runs up the wall and around the ceiling, and when it hits the smoke detector: BEEP, BEEP, BEEP!"

"Let's hope we get a 'Beep' not a 'Dink,' like we did at the smoke detector store," said Robbie.

"Father is putting the smoke detector close to our bedrooms. I'm sure we will hear the alarm in case of fire," said Jill.

"Remember, the smoke will not wake us up. In fact, the smoke will put us into a deeper sleep," Mr. Martin reminded the children.

"When we hear the alarm, we never pull the covers over our head or hide in the closet," said Jill.

"We should crawl out of bed, go to our bedroom door, and feel it," said Robbie.

"What if the door is hot?" asked Mr. Martin.

"Never open a hot door," exclaimed Jill.

"Go to your second escape route," said Robbie.

"The window!" both children shouted.

"And what are my rules on windows?" asked Mr. Martin.

"Never break a window. Learn how to open it," said Robbie.

"And never jump from a high window. Throw down an escape ladder or wait to be rescued by the firefighters," said Jill.

"Go to your family meeting place to see that everyone is safe, and never go back into a burning building, "said Robbie.

"Well, I can see you remembered your lessons," said Mr. Martin as he finished installing the Littlest Smoke Detector on the ceiling.

"All that's left to do is test this little guy," said Mr. Martin.

As Mr. Martin reached for the test button, all the bad memories from Burnie's came rushing back to the little smoke detector. He was sure the big smoke detectors were wrong about him. He could protect his new family from smoke and fire, but he was about to be tested. Mr. Martin pushed the button.

"DINK! DINK! DINK!"

I'm a failure, the Littlest Smoke Detector thought. The children had so much faith in me, and I have disappointed them and ruined the birthday party. "I told you he sounded puny," said Robbie.

"Be quiet," exclaimed Jill.

"Now, children," said Mr. Martin. "Let's test him every week to see if he gets louder. Then we will decide what to do."

Mr. Martin was not disappointed with his present, but he knew the Littlest Smoke Detector would have to be replaced if he could not get any louder.

As weeks went by, there was no change. Each time Mr. Martin tested the Littlest Smoke Detector, the same thing happened: "DINK! DINK! DINK!"

Mr. Martin called the children, "I'm afraid we have to get a new smoke detector," he said. The children were sad, but they knew he was right. "We can go in the morning to Burnie's." The Littlest Smoke Detector wanted what was best for the Martin family. In the morning, he would be replaced with a big smoke detector, one that could wake everyone up in case of smoke and fire.

The house soon turned dark. Everyone went to sleep, everyone except the Littlest Smoke Detector. This would be his last night in the Martin home, but he still had a job to do.

"Tomorrow, I will be taken back to the smoke detector store. I hope I have one more quiet night. But something was not right! My sensors are picking up something. Could it be SMOKE?"

There was no doubt about it. The Martin home was on fire! "I have to wake everyone, but will they hear me?" The Littlest Smoke Detector had no time to lose. He knew every second counts in a fire. He summoned every bit of strength he had in his little battery.

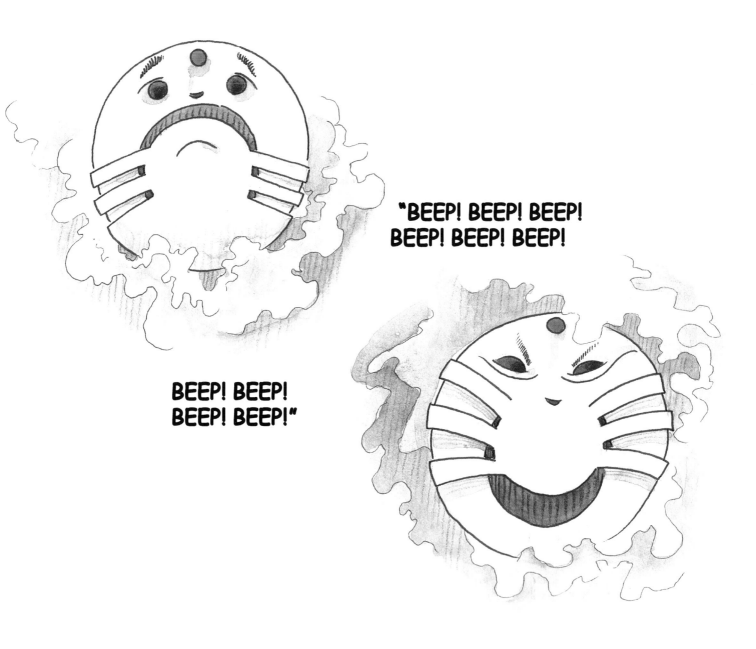

"BEEP! BEEP! BEEP! BEEP! BEEP! BEEP!

BEEP! BEEP! BEEP! BEEP!"

The Littlest Smoke Detector had done his job! He could not believe how much noise he was making. The Martins rushed from their beds. Mr. Martin grabbed Jill and Robbie by the hand. "Hurry, we must get out immediately," Mr. Martin said. The children were very frightened, but they had practiced their home fire-escape plan many times before and knew exactly what to do.

"Crawl low under the smoke, that's where the good air is," shouted Jill.

As they left the house, they went straight to the family meeting place: the mailbox.

"Is everyone safe?" asked Mr. Martin. The children were very frightened, but nodded their heads yes.

"I'm going to our neighbor's house to call 9-1-1. You children wait here until I return," Mr. Martin said.

The children were indeed safe, but something else occupied their thoughts. They could still hear the sound of the Littlest Smoke Detector. He was still "Beep, beep, beeping."

"That smoke detector saved our lives," said Robbie.

"I just knew he was a hero," said Jill

The sound of sirens soon filled the air.

"I can't hear the smoke detector anymore," said Jill as the fire trucks pulled in front of their house.

Jill and Robbie watched as the firefighters pulled hose from the fire engine. The firefighters, in full protective gear, pulled the heavy hose into their house. Within minutes, the fire was out.

Mr. Martin joined the children as the fire chief spoke to them. "I sure was glad to see you children out of the house. You must have practiced your home-escape plan," he said.

"Yes, we do," said Mr. Martin, "including a new smoke detector the children had just bought me for my birthday."

The children told the fire chief how they were going to replace the little smoke detector the next day, and how he had never before made enough noise to wake anyone up, until tonight, that is.

The fire chief was impressed by the story of the little smoke detector. As the last bit of smoke was removed from the Martin's home, the fire chief looked for the Littlest Smoke Detector. He directed a beam of light from his flashlight to a sound he heard from the ceiling. The sound was coming from the Littlest Smoke Detector. It was not a beep or even a dink. The little smoke detector could only make a "BUZZZZZZZ" sound. The Littlest Smoke Detector looked very different than he had looked before the fire. You see, in a fire, it can get very hot, especially up high near the ceiling. The little smoke detector had melted, and his wires burned.

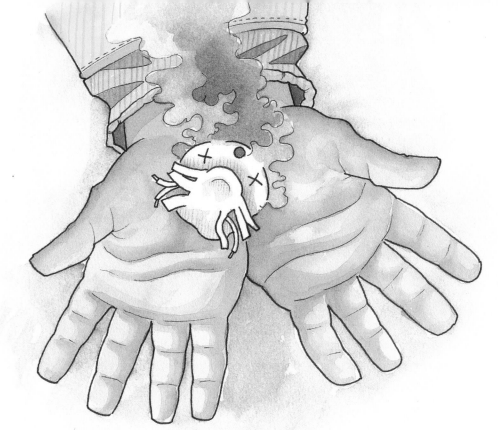

The fire chief moved down the hall with Mr. Martin. *Are they going to take me down already?* thought the Littlest Smoke Detector. The fire chief took a screwdriver from his pocket, and the little smoke detector was gently taken down.

"The fire chief has something to ask you," Mr. Martin said to the children.

The children were shocked to see how the little detector looked.

"I would like to take this smoke detector to the fire station with me, "said the chief.

"But why?" asked Jill.

"I think we should keep him to remind us just how important smoke detectors are, and the damage fire can do," said the chief. He added, "We can learn a lot from this smoke detector. I would like to tell everyone the story of the Littlest Smoke Detector, and take him to every school. Then everyone can learn just how important a good, working smoke detector is and how this detector saved your lives."

Jill and Robbie knew right away that this was the best thing to do.

"If more people knew about the Littlest Smoke Detector, they might buy new detectors and test their old ones more often," said Jill.

The chief just smiled as he carefully placed the little detector in his big pocket.

It was sad for the Littlest Smoke Detector to leave Jill and Robbie, but this was a new and exciting job. Now he travels everywhere with the fire chief, and everywhere he goes, people will hear the story of the Littlest Smoke Detector.

CPSIA information can be obtained
at www.ICGtesting.com
Printed in the USA
LVIC06n1447090114
368757LV00001BA/1

9 781425 960964